BIGGETY BAT

Hot Diggety, It's Biggety!

by Ann Ingalls
Illustrated by Aaron Zenz

SCHOLASTIC INC.

For Dad, who took me to the library. —A.I.

I found a friend in John Sandford!
Hot Diggety! —A.Z.

ISBN 978-0-545-66263-5
Text copyright © 2014 by Ann Ingalls
Cover and interior art copyright © 2014 by Aaron Zenz

Published by Scholastic Inc. SCHOLASTIC and associated logos are trademarks and/or registered trademarks of Scholastic Inc.

12 11 10 9 8 7 6 5 4 3 2 1   14 15 16 17 18 19/0

Printed in the U.S.A.   40
First printing, September 2014

Book design by Maria Mercado

As the sun went down in the west,
a bat named Biggety left his nest.

He was looking for a friend.

Down by the water
Biggety Bat heard
someone whoop—

WULLA! WULLA!

Who could it be?

EGRETS!
Scooping up some fish.

"Hot diggety!" said Biggety. "Egrets have friends, but… what about me?"

On the riverbank
Biggety Bat heard
someone splash —

SPLISH! SPLISH!

Who could it be?

TORTOISE!
Nibbling on a plant.

"Hot diggety!" said Biggety.
"Tortoise has friends, but...
what about me?"

Near the stony path
Biggety Bat heard
someone drone—

HUMM! HUMM!

Who could it be?

BEETLES!
Chasing down the ants.

"**Hot diggety!**" said Biggety.
"Beetles have friends, but . . .
what about me?"

By the tall lamppost
Biggety Bat heard
someone tweet —

PREET! PREET!

Who could it be?

MOCKINGBIRDS!

Singing so sweet.

"Hot diggety!" said Biggety. "Mockingbirds have friends, but . . . what about me?"

Above a park bench
Biggety Bat heard
someone chatter—

CHI! CHI!

Who could it be?

POSSUM!
Bearing babies home.

"Hot diggety!" said Biggety.
"Possums have friends but...
what about me?"

Back under his bridge
Biggety Bat heard
someone purr—

KRRR!

KRRR!

Who could it be?

RACCOON KITS!

As the moon rose full and bright,
Kits called, "Come play tonight."

"Hot diggety!" said Biggety.

BATS UNDER A BRIDGE

Biggety is a Mexican free-tailed bat. More than a million bats like him live under a bridge in Austin, Texas.

They sleep during the day. But at night, they eat insects that fly. People come to watch the bats. It is quite a show!

ANIMALS IN THIS BOOK

Snowy Egret

Gopher Tortoise

Green Tiger Beetle

Mockingbird

Possum

Raccoon